Changed
ANGRY HEARTS

Janae' Lachelle

authorHOUSE®

AuthorHouse™
1663 Liberty Drive
Bloomington, IN 47403
www.authorhouse.com
Phone: 1 (800) 839-8640

Published by AuthorHouse   09/20/2018

ISBN: 978-1-5462-4074-7 (sc)
ISBN: 978-1-5462-4073-0 (e)

Changed is dedicated to my children, god children, students and every Angry Heart of Chester, PA. young or old. It is time to execute CHANGE for the better regardless of PRIDE, RACE, or RELIGION.

A huge thanks to GOD, my editors Semika Roten, Jayne Thompson of Widener University, my cover designer Kareem Devine owner and CEO of DevineTOUCH & CO, my family, two of the best uncles John Barley and Terrance Avery with annual motivation, encouragement and prayers. The good friends, associates and my students of Chester High School.

Am I Next?

Michelle couldn't help but to feel worried in a neighborhood where someone is killed or shot everyday by someone of the same race. Every time I made it to school or home I would say the word "Safe" in my head. I mean it really feels like I'm running a marathon for life every day, while traveling to and from any destination in Chester, Pa. I wish I never watched the news the day of Sandra Blands' arrest and death because I'm supposed to visit my family in the same state come summer. The report gave me a whole new cause for worry after Trayvon Martins death.

Police are killing us without proper grounds and are getting away with it. I'm only thirteen years old, I shouldn't be worried about any police officer who took an oath to protect and serve their community. I'm a female who fears her own race and police officers. I can't help but to ask am I next in either situation. Many are killed as an innocent bystander when it comes to the streets. Many are killed by police officers for being an African American male or female across the country.

I do plan on attending college and having a life outside of Chester Pa. I have an essay due and I choose the title "AM I NEXT?", because my mom couldn't answer the question for me regarding what am I supposed to do if a black male or police officer is standing in front of me pointing a gun. Maybe my English teacher could give me an answer. On Monday, as I prepared to present my essay, my teacher handed me my essay and said "I wish I had an answer."

The look on my face showed of disappointment because after my research, I learned my rights and some laws but I thought my teacher would be able to clarify what my chances are in life. My mother's advice was to stay out of trouble when it comes to the law and I won't have to worry about the police. In some cases the young men and women weren't doing much for a police officer to take their life. As for the streets, I'm not supposed to be a follower only a leader, stay away from cliques, and not mind the boys because they aren't sure of their own needs at my age.

After school, I arrived home safe. .As I entered the house, my mom approached me saying "I have some answers to the question you asked," Am I Next?" Have a seat and listen sweetheart. Situations in the world have gotten worse but you have to remain focused and full of hope. With all you plan to do and become in life, please don't let our country's nonsense stop you now or ever. I don't know if you're the next Sandra Bland but I do know you can be the next to help defend, educate, and rebuild a community for a better tomorrow. It's all in what we're pursuing to help all people and reacting smarter not angrily. Please think about how your intelligence could help defend, educate and rebuild our community.

Well mom these situations surrounding me made me want to change my future goals, I no longer want to be a veterinarian but I will donate to help all endangered animals. After looking long and hard I decided to become a civil/criminal lawyer so I can help the human race not just mine become better.

Blithe (BLIYTH), adjective
Lightheartedness to the point of indifference or
uncaring; happily unconcerned and oblivious.

Blithe

by

Janae' Lachelle Avery

NEW HOME

*L*ora was a ten year old very intelligent only child. One day Lora's mother, Janice, told her their move was a definite. Lora had so many questions. "Mommy, will there be other little girls my age, will there be parks, and can we plant a garden oh and go to church?" Lora's mother replied, "Baby Girl where we're moving will be very different than where you have been. Times are hard and mommy has to do what she has to do just to keep a roof over your head. When I finish school we will find something better, I promise."

Two weeks went by and Lora's mother was on the move and the boxes were packed. "Lora honey, I need you to get to the car the truck is already packed. Are you ready?" Lora replied, yes mom. As Lora walked to the car she couldn't help but to look back at the lovely garden in the big yard and say Mommy this house was very pretty and huge. So off they went riding to their new home. As they arrived Lora asked her mother why are all these people standing around and look at those girls dance, what kind of dancing is that? Her mother responded with the kind you're not allowed to do, Lora listen to me you have to have a mind of your own be a leader never a follower. I hear you mom.

Alright well we're here, said Janice, this is our new home. Mom it's small and who is this lady approaching the car? I don't know but get out and say hello. Hello I'm Janice, hey J I'm Margie and I've been waiting on you all morning. Janice replied excuse me you called me J. Margie said, well I usually just call some by their first initial but I can tell by the look of you and your little girl you have class or money. She's a very pretty little girl. Is she mixed with Indian or Caucasian? Without waiting for a response Margie continued, her hair is beautiful, well let me tell you now the little girls around here won't like her and you better keep her on your front porch. Janice replied are you serious?

Janice figured it would be different but Margie was a bit more than she had expected. Lora also thought, *my goodness, Ms. Margie is too funny and she was all in our boxes and in return said now that's nosy. Janice spoke up with hey little lady stay in a child's place. While they were getting settled, Janice let Lora know a couple of guest would be arriving. Janice stated Uncle Reid and Pop-pop will be here shortly to set up our furniture. She then asked Lora if she was hungry and told her if so eat the lunch I packed for you.*

Shortly afterwards, the guests knocked on the door. Janice was happy they arrived safely .She greeted them and said welcome dad and Uncle Reid let me show you to our bedrooms so you guys can get started. Less than five minutes went by before there was another knock at the door. "Mom, Lora yelled some little girls are at the door for me!" Janice told Lora to hold on while she came downstairs. As Janice came down the staircase, Lora opened the door. Janice being slightly disturbed by that said, excuse you Lora never open the door without me saying so. Hello Lora says to the four girls but only one of the girls said hello. Lora's mother said hello to the girls in a louder voice and all four of the little girls spoke.

Meet The Neighbors

*L*ora's mother introduced herself by saying, I'm Mrs. Janice and this is my daughter Lora. Then she asked the girls what their names were. The first to politely respond was Kiah. While she pointed to a grey house she said, "Hi Mrs. Janice my name is Kiah; I live in that house across the street." The next person to address Janice was Daionna by saying I'm Daionna and I live down the street. Keya gave an introduction for herself and Amiyah. "I'm Keya and that's my best friend Amiyah but we call her Miyah, we live around the corner." Lora saw the approval on her mother's face and said to the girls, well okay do you want to play with me? They all answered yes.

Janice pulled Lora to the side before she left and warned her to keep an eye on Keya and Amiyah. The girls went off to play outside and out of nowhere Amiyah yelled, "First!" Keya quickly yelled "second!"

Lora wasn't sure what was taking place so she asked what kind of game is this? Kiah said jump rope, can you jump double Dutch? Lora didn't think she would jump very well but she told the girls she watched double Dutch competitions on TV. Keya and Miyah laughed loudly at Lora. Kiah told Lora she could take her turn third and she and Daionna will take the ends.

Daionna stared at the sisters and said that's not funny. Daionna said to Miyah you just learned. Shut up Daionna said Keya! Lora was shocked so she asked Keya, why did you tell your friend to shut up? "My mom can't stand those words" said Lora. Keya came back at Lora with well I'm not your mom! Lora started to think about what her mom just said about being a leader and to keep an eye on the best friends. Lora's next thought was that a parent can read friends. Lora told the girls she was going back into the house. Kiah and Daionna asked if they could come, Lora said sure.

As they walked towards Lora's house Keya and Miyah yelled y'all are two faced! Lora we want our fair one! Lora stopped and asked Kiah what is a fair one? Kiah said they want to fight you. Lora was puzzled and asked, what did I do? Kiah explained that she had fought with them so many times and Daionna had fought them too. Lora asked why are you still friends with them if you're always fighting each other. Daionna said Kiah taught me to forgive so I try; I only come outside if Kiah is out because they're good for jumping people. They get it from their moms. As the girls enter Lora's house, Lora told her mom what just happened.

Lora's mom says give me a minute and I'm going to talk to their parents. Janice told Lora to stay in the house and invited Daionna and Kiah for dinner. "Do you girls want some dinner?" Yes the girls replied. Kiah mentioned that she doesn't eat pork. Janice instructed the girls to ask their parents. After dinner, Janice asked Kiah and Daionna, if they could show herself and Lora where Keya and Miyah lived. The girls agreed. As Janice and all the girls arrived at the first house a young boy yelled from the porch, mom some lady is out here and she's fly too.

When the woman reached the front door, Janice introduced herself and Lora. As Lora was telling her side of the story Keya entered yelling snitches, Lora started it! Keya's mother hollered, shut up before I knock your teeth down your throat. Keya began crying and continued walking into the house. Keya's mom said to Janice neither of us was there so we don't know what happened, and then asked did my daughter hit yours? Janice said no and I don't want it to lead to that, that's why I'm here but trust me I understand and you don't have to worry about mine enjoy your night. As Janice walked Kiah and Daionna home the girls told her how drugs and men are always in both Keya's and Miyah's houses.

As they arrived at Daionna house, Janice met Daionna's mother and told her she had a nice house and a well-mannered daughter. They exchanged phone numbers and agreed to talk tomorrow. When they arrived at Kiah's house, Janice could smell incense burning and noticed a huge picture of Mecca hanging on the wall. Kiah's father gave Janice a heads up about the area. Janice told him how his daughter was well mannered. By this time Janice decided not to go to Amiyah's at this time.

While Lora and her mother were headed home two ladies were walking towards them and one happened to be Keya's mother. As they walked past each other Keya's mom said to the lady with her, "Yeah she thinks she's all that, please!" Lora says mom was she talking to you? Janice says No did she mention my name? That's what *you call bleak and indirect speaking, if you don't see me feeding into that you shouldn't either Baby Girl. Let's have a movie night in our new home. Lora replied that's what I'm talking about mom!*

Being Forgiving

*A*s Lora prepared for their first movie night in the new house, she took a shower. When she finished, she said to her mother, we have to pray for Keya, Miyah and their family because I don't want to fight even if they're mean and thoughtfully added, I miss my friends! Lora's mom said well-baby girl praying is a must and I'm not raising you to be a physical fighter or a troublemaker but sometimes we have to defend ourselves in physical ways because of the way others treat us. Keep in mind if you can't help them then stay away from them.

The next morning Lora was awakened to the smell of breakfast. It was her favorite, French toast, smelling delicious as she headed downstairs. With a smile she entered the kitchen to say good morning mom, I love you! Janice smiled back at her and said good morning baby, I love you too. Janice asked Lora how she slept. Lora answered, It was good, I dreamed of our old house.

Do you remember my sleepovers they were so much fun. "Lora you can still have sleepovers," said Janice. Lora started considering a sleepover.

She asked her mother, "Who would I invite; school doesn't start for another two months." Janice said you don't have to wait until school starts. We're pretty much unpacked so how about you have one tonight? Are you serious mom then yes I can't wait to get dressed so I can ask the girls? So far Kiah and Daionna are invited. Lora went upstairs to get dressed. As she peeked out of her bedroom window she saw Daionna headed to her house and said good morning lady I'm on my way out now. Lora's mom yelled for her to stay out of the window!

Lora headed outside and offered Daionna some sunflower seeds. Lora asked would you like to come to my sleepover tonight. Daionna replied, yes but I have to ask my mom. Awe man Keya is coming! Lora turned around to say good morning Keya! Keya looked very surprised but said good morning Lora! Daionna mentioned the sleepover. Keya asked if she was invited. Lora said I have to ask my mom because of what happened yesterday but my mom doesn't carry drama into the next day so it may be a yes. Will you invite Miyah asked Keya?

Of course I will. I have to talk to Kiah so I can ask

her too. Keya retreated to get Miyah. Lora knocked on Kiah's door and her father answered. Lora said good afternoon sir, can Kiah come outside? I'm inviting her to my sleepover tonight if she's allowed. You can speak to my mom if you need details. Well after I talk to your mother I don't see why not. Kiah will be out after she's dressed. As the girls were leaving Kiah's house talking about the sleepover they noticed Keya and Miyah headed to Lora house with bags and blankets. Daionna asked so Mrs. Janice said it was fine?

Lora told the girls, I haven't asked my mom yet. Keya blurted out well our moms said it was fine and that your mom seems cool and we're sorry about yesterday. Lora goes in the house asking the girls to wait outside for her. Mom you're not going to believe this but do you remember our pastor saying love your neighbors? Yes I do! I spoke to Keya this afternoon she spoke back to me in addition, she and Miyah apologized about yesterday so I invited them to my sleepover. Lora I'm proud of you all but I'll go around and speak to all parents for permission later.

After Lora expressed her impatience with a sigh, she explained that Keya and Miyah's mothers said its fine and that you seemed cool. They're out front with clothes

& blankets! Oh really, I'll still stop by just to make sure. As Lora opened the door to invite them in they said Hello Mrs. Janice she replied hello ladies sit your things over by the dining room entrance. I will still stop pass your houses just to make sure it's okay with your mothers. We're sorry about yesterday Keya spoke looking into Janice's eyes, that's fine I'm a forgiver sweetheart. We're all going to church tomorrow except Kiah due to her religion but she will still enjoy the sleepover!

Mom did you know that Kiah is my first Muslim friend I think she looks beautiful with her Kimar on! Thank you Lora, other kids' tease me but they just don't understand stand Islam. Ok little ladies what's on the menu for dinner tonight Janice asked? They all yelled pizza except Keya she yelled crabs. Janice laughed and told the girls to go play nice because it was still early. I will talk to all of your parents later.

When the girls got outside they discussed past experiences at sleepovers and religion. Lora told them her mom was going to do their nails, make popcorn, and play games. Keya said and church tomorrow oh my God as she shook her head in disbelief. Miyah said save your praise for tomorrow I think I been to church like two times unless I went when I was a baby besides Keya *no one else invited us to sleepovers. Daionna mentioned going to church often with her grandmother but said her parents barely go so my grandma says to my parents "you shouldn't just send Dai, but attend yourself".*

Lora added I have been going to church before I could walk. Lora asked Kiah how she worshipped. Well we attend the Mosque every Friday no shoes are to be worn and when my dad calls me in the house throughout the day we have prayer, oh we don't eat pork either, I'm a Salafi Muslim. Well my mom won't feed me pork either said Lora. Lora yelled let's play rope 1st! Keya was 2nd, Daionna 3rd, Kiah and Miyah has the ends. Kiah said "alright Lora just jump in when this side go down" and she did, the girls cheered her on saying, "Go Lora!" Kiah said that was me not too long ago.

As the girls finished jumping rope Lora said thank you so much for teaching me how to jump double Dutch! You're always saying thank you and good morning Keya replied. If I didn't show manners to others my mom would have a fit blah blah. Well a fit is better than a hit, do your mom even cuss asked Keya? Yes she does but not around me, I usually hear her over the phone laughing with my aunt. Daionna said I don't get beatings, I have been popped a couple times but now just punishment.

Yeah me too said Kiah. Miyah just shook her head & said I don't get beatings but my mom yells a lot and sometimes that can hurt.

Keya said remember we got caught stealing Miyah your mom whipped your butt, Ok Ok! Let's take turns pushing each other but first Lora I'm really sorry about yesterday and I don't like to fight, I thought you were being smart and was going to take my friends away from me. Lora replied no way I would like to have some new friends, I don't like to fight but I know how, my dad showed me before he died. My mom said if she's not fighting then I shouldn't be fighting, that's not our thing (laughing)! Miyah commented that Lora would meet new friends when school started in a couple of months.

Learning One Another

Kiah told Lora that she was sorry to hear about her dad, you don't have to talk about it. Lora said no it's fine, he got sick it was so fast but I loved our times together and I want to make him proud of me. I cry sometimes but my mom makes it better by being there. Kiah went on to say I love having my abee (father), he is the best but I don't have an ummi (mother), not at this time and I barely get to talk to her or even write her replied Kiah. Where does she live, doesn't she have a cell phone? Keya asked.

You weren't listening when your mom told my mom that her mom is in jail Miyah said. Lora grabbed Kiah's hand and told her we can be there for each other since it can be sad at times, for some reason many in the world don't want Muslims and Christians to be there for one another but we'll show them! Hey we're missing our daddies too mine is in jail, my mom said that's his second home but my dad said he was just trying to feed us said Keya. Miyah said her father is in the Navy and when he gets off that ship he's going to buy her everything. Lora told Kiah if it was anything she could do to help her reach out to her mom then so be it. Kiah said we write each other letters and I get to talk to her some. I also visit once a month with my abee (father).

"Lora!" yelled her mom "time for lunch and would the girls like to join you?" They all said yes. So little ladies how about some chicken fingers and French fries, wash your hands and have a seat anywhere it's the same on each plate. Keya says Mrs. Janice you're a good mom and how did you get that way? Well lady any blessings from God you're supposed to cherish and be thankful for also treating all people around you regardless of color or religion with respect is you being a blessing to you both. Sometimes people are disrespectful but that doesn't mean join in because then you're disrespectful right along with them and you shouldn't want that.

As the girls sat at the table eating they begin to look around at each other, Keya said I want my mom to start treating me and my brothers as a blessing. Miyah said me too; we have to pray right Lora and Kiah? Yes said Lora and Kiah! Janice walks in the kitchen to ask how *lunch was. "Delicious" said the girls. You may also have an ice cream cone then I'll go confirm the sleepover with your parents.*

Each One Teach One

The girls grabbed their ice cream and headed back outside as they walked towards the park Miyah and Keya notice Lay-Lay. Miyah said hold up ladies Lay-Lay is at the park and I don't want to fight today, I have this peace thing going on and it feels good. Keya said me too I feel like a newborn baby and I'm happy. Lay-Lay is a big trouble maker! Daionna, Lora, and Kiah looked at them and said "WHAT?!" at the same time. Kiah said you both are always starting with us but Lay-Lay is a big trouble maker.

Keya said she is very disrespectful, once she threw water ice on me and we fought well she beat me up but I was just trying to defend the disrespect I guess. Miyah said well she smacked me for nothing and took my jump rope. Don't forget your sunflower seeds too Keya said. Miyah mentioned that it was Lay-Lay's friends Dimples and Shi-Shi that took the sunflower seeds. Lora said why didn't you tell your mom's? Keya replied we did and they told us to beat her up or pick up something and bust her in the head.

Guess my mom wanted me to be really disrespectful, I just want her to leave me alone. Lora said that's probably why you pick on us, my mom talked to me about this because of bullying at my old school and it was a private school. My mom regrets sending me there but she said bullying and other violence is sometimes imitated. Miyah asked what is imitating and can we go to jail for it? Lora laughed and said yes if you break the law and I will explain. Because of all that Lay-Lay does to you, now you do to others and it could go on but we're not going to feed the blithe meaning. Miyah before you ask just ignore the uncaring Lay-Lay! Yes she needs prayers. Keya said. Daionna said well let's go and see if it works. Keya said Kiah and Lora start praying now.

Thank God she's not with the rest of what you called blithe. Kiah it's a lot more blithe people where she's from. As the girls approached the park Lay-Lay yelled "HEY small head bald head!" None of the girls said a word. Then Lay-Lay yelled "All the Dirt balls!" Still no one spoke a word. Lay-Lay started walking away from the park looking back sticking her tongue out and rolling her *eyes. By the time she was down the street the girls busted out laughing and Kiah, Keya, Miyah, and Daionna said to Lora you're a blessing to us and Lora replied you have to remain blasé to blithe meaning unbothered.*

Prayers Work

T he sleepover was a success. The girls enjoyed being pampered by Mrs. Janice and of course Ms. Margie helped out as well. Pizza and crabs was on the menu and a long night of popcorn and movies. Kiah and Lora taught the girls a little bit about Islam and Christianity. They all went to church on Sunday including Kiah where she was welcomed with open arms. Thanks to her father for teaching her that no religion should teach hate.

When the girls got to their own households they shared the word with their parents and siblings about church and how not to feed the blithe. Eventually Keya and Miyah's mothers thanked Janice and apologized for their bleak attitudes. The moms spoke of visiting her church next week and they did. Keya's mom gave a testimony of how men and drugs kept her from being a mother but when her daughter came home asking for her to be a blessing to her she was speechless and couldn't wait to return with all three of her children.

Miyah's mother followed Keya's mom as usual. She also goes to church and is spending more time at home with her children. Both mother's started working at a local nursing home where they will be attending classes for their C.N.A license. Daionna's parents are now joining her and her grandma for church on Saturday's, they're also doing a lot more as a family.

The following Friday Lora, Daionna, Miyah, and Keya joined Kiah as she took her Shahada at Mosque. Keya told Kiah's abee (father) aren't you glad your feet don't stink! He just looked away shaking his head. Lora and her mom spoke of their new home, Janice told Lora how proud she was of her and to stay positive keeping God first. By the way, school will start soon Lora. Are you ready?

Our Sons & Guns

by

Janae' Lachelle Avery

Our Sons And Guns

I grew up without either parent. My mom tried raising me, but she was caught up in the streets. She barely cooked or had hugs and kisses. My dad was in and out of jail. When he was out, he played house with other women and their children. So I had to basically raise myself. When I turned thirteen, everything changed: my friends, my grades and even my heart. I didn't have a care in the world and neither did my four homies: Marvin (Marv), Lafenus (Fenny), Ardel (Arty) and Carl (Cees). My name is Anthony (Tough Tony).

We all consider ourselves brothers from another. By the time we were sixteen, we had already stolen cars and broken into people's houses. Only Marv

& Cees have been to juvenile detention centers and based on Marv's description, it was no place for us. Cees thought differently. He considered it fun and said, "They care more about me than my own family."

I never could understand why Fenny even hung around us. He had both parents at home, was well cared for, he had the hottest gear, and was known as a sneaker head. That didn't stop him from being a thief. Arty came from a good home too but his mother worked so much to keep a roof over their heads that she was never home and probably wouldn't think of Arty breaking into people's houses. We enjoyed girls and money until we went to a party and Marv was all over some dude's girl - not just any dude. His name was Sam and he was from 9th Street.

The 9th Street guys were heavily into guns, money, and drugs. During the party, we were surrounded by all of them. As Sam approached Marv, I could see it in Marv's eyes. He was scared. I remember hearing Sam say, "You ain't about this life," and then the gunshots rang out. It was dark so we couldn't see what was going on - just fire from guns and the smell of gun smoke. I remembered getting up off the floor and seeing Arty lying there shot, blood everywhere and him yelling, "Call my mom. Get me some help. I don't want to die!"

I was in shock. I couldn't move, but by then the police and ambulance were there. The police took me to the station and questioned me, but I honestly didn't see who shot Marv [you can't tell what you didn't see]. Sam wasn't the only one with a gun out of his homies. As my aunt picked me up from the police station, all I kept hearing was Arty saying, "I don't want to die". By the time I got home, I realized I didn't want to die either, but Marvin and Cees had other plans. When I got in the house, Marv & Cees were sitting on the couch asking me questions just like the police.

Then Cees pulled out a gun and said, "If Arty don't make it, we all gonna be bout that life because it's either us or them." Call me what you want, but when I saw the gun, tears rolled down my face and I said, "I don't want to die." Marv's phone rang and Sam's girl told him that Sam and his homies were at the gas station talking about what they were going to do to us. Cees said to Marv, "Not now. Cops are out and we need more guns. I have to call my old head at the store."

I thought to myself, thank you God, what just happened, why us?! The next morning I got a call that Arty was in the Intensive Care Unit (I.C.U). He had been shot four times: twice in the chest, once in the right arm, and once in the leg. I was so hurt from what I was told. I called Fenny, but I didn't get an answer. Then I heard a knock at my door. It was Marv. He walked in and pulled his shirt up to show two guns on his hips.

All I could do was shake my head. Then he said, "Remember how you used to beat the whole block up when we were young? Tony, you were not scared of anybody, not even Sam." "Marv, I fought with my hands, not a gun. That's a huge difference. I want to live to see a better life other than what my mom and pop had to offer me. Let me think, Marv. I'm about to go see Arty at the hospital."

Marv said, "Well, I'm not running scared. You can't protect yourself with your fist and they all carry guns, real shooters!" As I arrived at Arty's room,

Fenny was leaving and said he saw who did it and his parents were sending him to his grandmother's until things cooled off. Right then and there, I knew Fenny wasn't going to be able to live here anymore since he was considered a witness, because the streets would consider him a snitch. I couldn't stand to see Arty with tubes all in him, with a machine helping him to breathe.

It brought tears to my eyes. I could only hope this humbled his mother and sat her down for a while because she was like my mom. I kissed her forehead and left. As I was going home, I noticed a blue car ride past me twice. Something didn't seem right, so I turned off the street and called Marv. But before I knew it, I was being shot at.

I counted twelve, but it was sixteen shots and I wasn't hit by one bullet. Now I'm back at the police station and the detectives had their own story, thinking we were beefing over drug territory, but since they had nothing on me they let me go. I bet if I took that gun Marv offered this could be going another route. Here comes my aunt again. She said "God was with you Tony."

She said, "I'm always praying for you and your

mother. All I can do now is thank the lord. This is the second time God saved you. Have you thanked him? Before you're taken away from us by incarceration or death, please attend church with your little sister. She's always asking for you." I thought to myself, if I told her that I did thank God the other night would she believe me?

By the time I got home I had twenty-two missed calls including texts. A few calls from my mom cussing me out but not asking if I was alright. I wanted to ask her, "Did I ask to be here?" If I had a choice, I may not have chosen her to be my mother. She never really was, but I forgive her. Out of all those calls, I wondered who really cares for me or did they just want something to gossip about?

I could hear Future's lyrics, "Shawty wasn't checking for me, Momma wasn't checking for me." I called Marv to tell him that I was good but mad and hurt inside. Once things like this start, it's only two ways you can end up, dead or in jail, as my aunt always said. I still did not want either, but what was I supposed to do. I wanted to make an honest living, become the father I never had, with a real woman as my wife.

I spent some time considering how I could change my outcome. No more robberies. I'll go into the Air Force. My uncle made good money and got a free college education. That's my ticket out of the hood so I can make it to church with my little sister and aunt. As I rose up off the floor, I realized I was praying.

Now I was regretting the name Tough Tony. I was still angry at the fact that I was shot at and my homie was laid in a hospital bed. I chose LIFE over death or incarceration. Needing a gun on your hip at all times is a dead man walking. That's a hard life to live. Sam was caught by police with two guns. One was the gun that shot Arty, but Sam didn't shoot Arty.

His so called right hand man did it and Sam told the police the story for a lighter sentence. What Sam didn't know was they already had a witness and warrants had been issued. Fenny was the witness, not a snitch. He wanted justice for his friend and only told what he seen. Arty is recovering well, up walking and talking.

Arty only remembers a little of what had happened that night. Cees was still keeping the chaos going in the street; he even got some young bulls to continue the beef with the 9th street gang because Marv was doing time now for a gun. Before me and Cees could visit him, Cees was shot and killed and it wasn't anyone from 9th street. The word on the streets is that one of Cees soldiers was just as hungry as he was and killed him for fifteen hundred dollars.

When I went to visit Marv, he had turned eighteen years old and became Muslim. He now goes by the name Ajas which means powerful, strong and purity. I saw and heard the change in him and even though we don't follow the same religion we keep each other focused through prayers, fasting, and meditation. I'll take a friend who prays five times a day over anyone else. I'm a Christian now and I speak to youth about violence and our situation because the newspaper told a story I knew nothing about. I tell the children the truth.

I will be leaving soon. I decided on the Army, heck free college, travel, and the only war I want to be a part of is to save our country, not to kill my own people. Marv agreed with me too. I considered for that time of prayer, God led me to a righteous life. I realized I wouldn't be young forever. Thinking before action is why I'm living and why I am free, only letting God guide me.

Say what you want, but God saved me and had better plans for me. I want all he has to offer. My days and nights are at ease. Marv/Ajas became an author in prison with a little help from me. I now understand that the Army is not for me. I'm done with war seems pointless period. So after I graduate college, I plan to become an educator or principle. I'll return home and work on saving our youth and teaching them all aspects of living to become better for themselves. Again I rise off my knees from praying and I can honestly say my life is better as a God fearing man!

Miracle Shoes

by

Janae' Lachelle Avery

Miracle Shoes

This grandbaby, Lillian, is someone special. As I look into her eyes I see a giver. When she's at my house she loves to walk around in my slippers that are ten times her size. I just sit back and smile! Hello Pop-pop its turkey day so Happy Thanksgiving and what are you thankful for? Her pop-pop looks down and says our family and the love I receive from you all. Thank God! Well I'm thankful for the same things. Thank you Jesus!

Lewis get the door shouted Lillian's Grandma Janie. Lillian your friend is at the door. Lillian greeted her friend. Hey Queeny Happy Thanksgiving! Same to you it smells good. Did your grandma bake a cake? Yes she did and a big turkey, stuffing, mac and cheese, greens, and cornbread. Awe man it's so much food Lillian stated. What did your mom cook Queeny?

We're having a regular dinner. Huh said Lillian? Well my parents didn't have enough money for all the usual food. My dad said we can't worry about one day when we need food for the days to come. Plus he had to work and won't be home until eleven at night. My pop-pop said be thankful for love and family. He didn't mention a turkey but if it makes you feel better come have dinner with us. No because it won't be fair to my little brother or sister and my mom will say no anyway.

My mom got upset earlier when my little sister asked about a turkey replied Queeny. Lillian said let me think of something...ok listen, when my family is finished eating you can meet me out back and I will give you all a Thanksgiving dinner so look at the light in the backyard I will flick the light three times and you come outside. Queeny just be thankful for this day, you did wake up and tell your mom to look at the homeless & ill people. Lillian time to eat, does Queeny want to join us? No pop-pop she is about to eat as well.

As Lillian sat at the table and the family began to pray and make declarations of what they were thankful for she couldn't take Queeny off her mind. Grandma the food was delicious and the cake was so yummy. Thank you! Awe suga you're welcome, there's so much food leftover...well better pack some food for your house or your dad will have a fit! Definitely because my mom is not such a good cook so my daddy does the cooking most of the time.

Child you better hush before your mother hears you (they both laugh).

As Lillian's grandma packed up the food there was still enough food to feed two more families. Lillian said to her grandma you still have too much food. Yes honey I know, we will send plates tomorrow too. Then Lillian asked her grandmother if she could stay the night? Sure! After the football game was over Lillian's family started to leave.

Lillian's cousin jokingly yelled goodnight bighead. Lillian retorted Oh be quiet, you were thankful for a PSP game silly! Alright Lillian you can get a bath and put your pajamas on, you still have time to watch television or the computer, and afterwards in the back room you go. I'll be back to pray with you said her pop-pop. Yes sir! When Lillian came out of the room she flew to the kitchen and prepared plates of food and desserts and hit the light switch three times. As she heard the back gate open it was Queeny and her little brother.

Oh my goodness Lillian what will I tell my mom? Tell her my pop-pop insisted plus he's always looking out for your family. Thank you so much Lillian and my mom felt so much better after I told her what I was thankful for. No problem I'll see you after breakfast tomorrow! Lillian returned to the living room as her pop-pop was coming downstairs. Time to pray sweetheart! After praying Lillian's pop-pop told her to always give unto God and never expect anything in return and I guarantee God will bless you for all your works for him here on earth!

Pop-pop what do you mean by give unto God? I always give at church Lillian replied. Well that's what church members do to help the church with all sorts of things but what I mean is giving to people no matter their race or religion something helpful and positive. Oh ok like a dinner that could help a family in need? Yes sweetheart, and from my understanding you're always taking things to school to give to other children. Your dad told me. She laughed and said yes a fairly new coat because a girl didn't have one and I have many.

See you already started your works for that man above and I have done the same so let's keep it going, love you and get some rest. Pancakes for breakfast! I love you too pop-pop goodnight! As morning arrived Lillian's grandma went into the kitchen to start breakfast. She opened the refrigerator and yelled "Lewis!" Lewis replied what's wrong Hun? "Where is half of the Thanksgiving dinner? Take a look in the fridge!" When Lewis opened the refrigerator he couldn't do anything but smile and say Janie, the question is who she gave it to.

Lewis looked around, checked the windows and doors, and he then called Lillian. Well Janie, you might as well go ahead and make breakfast as he kissed her forehead we have a freezer full of meats. I'll cook dinner tonight if need be don't worry. Lewis that child will give the clothes off her back, I just pray that no one ever takes advantage of her; she is so sweet and sincere. Lewis I tell you our grandbaby is here for a reason, make sure she didn't give the freezer away.

Let me take this trash out, here she comes. She must smell those pancakes cooking. As Lewis walked out back his neighbor was standing at the gate with a big smile. Good morning Mr. Lewis I just want to thank you and Mrs. Janie for our Thanksgiving dinner. My family was very happy and with me working long hours with only enough money to pay the mortgage our meals are a little lighter but my children eat three times a day and they have clean clothes. "I sure hope the fire department calls me soon I passed my exams...I Thank you for that as well said Queeny's dad Carl."

Lewis shared with Carl, son there is no explanation needed I understand and have been down that road before but after I gave it to God my life changed for the better. The fire department will be calling you soon. I was a firefighter for 25 years and before that I walked in many shoes. Just don't give up Carl those children need you and so does your wife. Carl was comforted and replied, I won't they're the reason I keep going and we'll be back to church soon. Lewis commented, well that's the best thing you can offer your family. The children may not understand completely now but they'll thank you later trust me. I'll talk to you later and if you need me for anything please don't hesitate and enjoy your day! You do the same sir. When Lewis returned to the house Lillian was sitting at the table eating her pancakes.

Good morning Pop-pop! I know, I know sorry for giving your Thanksgiving dinner away. Sweetie you have nothing to be sorry for, that was giving unto God and I would have done the same thing but I didn't know. Mr. Carl is very thankful. Lillian said so is Queeny and next time I'll let you know first. Lewis started coughing so Janie reminded him to take his medicine.

Pop-pop are you sick? Lillian I am but I'm only eating right sometimes. I just need to improve my eating habits more, we all do! Does my daddy know? Yes he does. You should let my mom show you healthy meals to make. She's a nutritionist and a vegetarian. My dad said that's her excuse for not being able to cook.

Later that day Lillian's parents came to take her home. Before she left she went out front to talk to Queeny. She asked Queeny how was your Thanksgiving. It was so much better than I expected especially for my little sister. Now she can honestly finish her report about her Thanksgiving holiday thanks to you. The fried turkey was delicious alone and with that strawberry cake even better! Your welcome Queeny!

I have to go home; maybe I'll come next weekend.

I'll call you. Lillian gave her grandparents big hugs and headed to the car. Put you seat belt on Lillian her mother said. Dad why didn't you tell me Pop-pop was sick? Well at your age I didn't want you to worry, he will be fine. What is he sick from, what is it called? If I tell you, you wouldn't know. Dad yes I will, that's what Google is for, so what is it? Lillian's dad responded, High blood pressure.

Lillian was shocked. Oh my goodness that is the leading cause of death for African Americans! Wait a minute how do you know and baby girl don't worry he takes his medicine so he will be fine her father said attempting to be consoling. My health teacher taught us about high blood pressure. You are paying for me to receive a good education. Those 4th grade teachers don't play at Echoes Academy said Lillian's mother.

Lillian's mom went on to say sweetie I'm your first teacher and if you start to eat the way I do you won't have to worry about illnesses or medication. You and your father can stop criticizing the way I eat and can cook because none of us need all that greasy food. By the way we're proud of you Lillian for paying attention in school. Mom, dad and I would love to taste the healthier foods you cook. Speak for yourself baby girl (laughing) but yes I will try some of the healthier meals my wife cooks.

Well say no more and I know you'll love it, I can make meals using chicken and fish but only fresh with no hormones and my lovely husband will clean all meats. I sure will. Mom and dad if it's ok with you can I spend the weekends I don't have karate with Pop-pop so I can monitor his eating habits? Yes you most certainly can baby girl her dad replied! Before the next weekend Lillian went to her grandparents' house, Lillian's dad received a phone call from Mr. Carl.

"Hi John, you need to get to the hospital, it's your father he had a stroke and your mother is with him on their way to the hospital. I'm watching the house, keep me posted on his condition." Awe man, Thank you Carl! The look on John's face made his wife Nicole question what's wrong John? My dad just had a stroke he's at the hospital. No, no, no daddy strokes aren't good Lillian replied with tears in her eyes! I know baby, come on let's get to the hospital.

Nicole please drive, John said more as a command than a request. The ride to the hospital was silent but Lillian cried non-stop then she yelled out, we have to pray, and they did. As they arrived at the hospital

John took note of the look on his mother's face filled with ongoing tears. Mom I'm here, John said as he held her tightly in his arms. She looked him in his eyes and whispered in his ear, I left your father at home only his flesh and bones are here. She squeezed her son tighter as he began crying harder.

Lillian and her mother wrapped their arms around both of them. Lillian said crying my Pop-pop said if he leaves us in this way he would be in a better place! Awe sweetheart I know said her grandma let me sit a minute son then I'll sign the papers, I need to see him before we leave. My dear husband, oh Lord I call on you for the strength to deal with his absence because I know Lewis lives in us all. Do you all hear me we have to be strong that's all he wants for us with dealing with his passing. Lewis made me promise to him that I would deliver this message "our strength will outlast this time of grief."

As they arrived at Lillian's grandparents' house more tears fell. Lillian ran upstairs to their bedroom and sat on the bed looking at her grandfather's shoe closet thinking of all the stories he told her about each pair of shoes, how he walked, marched, and used them for work. When her father came into the room she looked at him and said Pop-pop wanted you to have those black shoes at the top those were his church shoes. Oh really?! Yes, he told me to find someone for each pair. Lillian's grandmother stood in the doorway and said yes he did.

John told Lillian to let her grandma get some rest, she's fine, that's all she does when she's here anyway. John said to his mother, Nicole and I will be in the next room if you need us. Ok baby goodnight. Lillian said goodnight daddy and instructed him to say his prayers. Her father agreed to do so. Grandma don't worry I'm going to take good care of you and I'm going to make sure I give those shoes to all the men that need them. Lillian your Pop-pop said you would do right by choosing the right men for those shoes. Those shoes made it throughout many trials indeed.

The day of the funeral Lewis' family and friends filled his house. Lillian couldn't help but to overhear her dad and Mr. Carl speak about how proud Lewis would be if he knew Carl passed the exam and got accepted as a firefighter. Carl stated, all I need is my boots and I'm ready. I hope Mr. Lewis knew the positive impact he had on my family and me. As

Lillian approached Mr. Carl she said if you don't mind me asking what size do you wear? Sweetie a size ten!

That's great my Pop-pop is a size ten as well and I have the perfect boots for you, barely worn. "It will be a pleasure having the complete protective gear. Now I can start active duty. I wouldn't want the fire chief to call me to work and I didn't have safety boots. Thank you so much Lillian!" As Carl was taking the boots his phone began ringing. Mr. Carl informed Lillian that it was the fire chief calling him to work a third shift for the night. Lillian encouraged Mr. Carl by telling him her Pop-pop would be proud and he should probably get some rest for the overnight shift as an active fire fighter.

As Lillian was coming down the steps to give Mr. Carl the boots she noticed a gentleman poking his finger in a young man's chest saying, "You are Muslim, Islam is your deen, the Quran is your life, and Allah is the light. You have acts of Kafir." As Lillian handed the boots to Mr. Carl, she tapped her dad and asked what are Muslims? Lillian they're followers of Islam a different religion. Pop-pop spoke of Islam. He said he marched with many of his brothers to save Mosques a long time ago.

Was Pop-pop a Muslim? Yes he was, they called him Sadar, and as you know your grandpa walked in many shoes and all of them were for righteousness and unity. He helped free communities in times of prejudice and injustice. The young man's father is trying to teach him a righteous path because the times have changed for the worst and we're losing too many young men in the streets for senseless situations. Our youth are quickly expiring by either dying or going to jail every day.

Lillian expressed to her father that she would like to introduce herself to the young man. She proceeded toward the young man and said hello. Lillian let him know her name and told him she was Mr. Lewis' grand-daughter. The young man returned the introduction by saying his name was Ahmad. Lillian engaged Ahmad in conversation after explaining she didn't want to be nosy. She then asked Ahmad was he in trouble. Ahmad replied, not really, I just don't understand why my dad is so strict on me when it comes to our religion.

Ahmad went on to say, "I try my hardest to stay on my deen but my dad doesn't recognize that. He wants me in the community sharing with my peers about Islam and when I do I'm considered weird or crazy". Ahmad continued by saying, he was fed up with not fitting in. In response, Lillian asked Ahmad if he had ever been to the local library. Of course Ahmad had been to the library but he let Lillian finish. Lillian explained that Ahmad's father joined her grandfather in a march to include an Islamic section in the library and it was successfully added at a time when they were considered crazy.

"What I'm saying is that you have to stand for your beliefs regardless of other opinions," said Lillian. Ahmad was shocked." Wow, my father helped to have the Islamic section of the library. He never told me." Lillian didn't understand why Ahmad's father hadn't shared that part of his Islamic history so she changed the subject. "Ahmad while you are here, I have some barely used oxford shoes I know my Pop-pop would love for you to have. What size do you wear?"

Ahmad said that he wears a size ten. "Perfect they are a size ten. I'll get the shoes while you talk to your father about his past and I will bet that you have a change of heart about his expectations regarding your religion." Before Lillian retreated, Ahmad told Lillian that he appreciated their conversation and the shoes.

He then offered his condolences for her loss. Lillian let Ahmad know that he was welcomed and told him to remember if he saved five out of ten young men from the streets, he would have done a great job.

When Lillian returned with the shoes, she entered the dining room and expressed to Ahmad's father, "we will never know where we're going unless we know where we came from". Ahmad's father had a look of gratitude on his face and told Lillian she was a wise soul. Lillian's father soon approached and told Lillian he would like to speak with her in the back yard. Lillian headed behind her father into the back yard. When Lillian reached the yard her father instructed her to have a seat on the swing facing him.

Lillian I grew up in these streets and it was hard but I had to think and make right decisions regarding who to be around and where to go for fun. I made mistakes along the way but not one to put me in jail or get me killed. If I didn't have my dad I don't know where I would be and I'm thankful for what you witnessed that man say to his son even poking him with his finger. I try my hardest as your father to make sure you won't have to experience situations that so many children are suffering through but you have to be willing to do what your mother and I expect of you or you will always learn lessons some being harder than others.

Dad I don't know what my future brings but so far you all are doing a good job demonstrating good ethics. Queeny's family and our neighbors at home say it takes a village to raise a child but if people don't know who they are or where they came from, how can they reach a child? Lillian's father began to explain the essence of unity and how breaking negative cycles in every household was so important to the next generation.

Maybe you should share Pop-pop's story of his marches with the young man, hearing it from you may help him understand his father and make a difference. As much as I wanted to give my grandfather's shoes away, it wasn't the shoes he left to uplift his village, but his words of wisdom. I will now share those words to all regardless of race or religion.

Printed in the United States
By Bookmasters

Printed in the United States
By Bookmasters